Cryptopedia

Andrew Demcak

NOMADIC PRESS

OAKLAND
111 FAIRMOUNT AVENUE
OAKLAND, CA 94611

BROOKLYN
475 KENT AVENUE #302
BROOKLYN, NY 11249

WWW.NOMADICPRESS.ORG

MASTHEAD

FOUNDING AND MANAGING EDITOR
J. K. FOWLER

ASSOCIATE EDITOR
MICHAELA MULLIN

DESIGN
J. K. FOWLER

MISSION STATEMENT

Nomadic Press is a 501 (C)(3) not-for-profit organization that supports the works of emerging and established writers and artists. Through publications (including translations) and performances, Nomadic Press aims to build community among artists and across disciplines.

SUBMISSIONS

Nomadic Press wholeheartedly accepts unsolicited book manuscripts. To submit your work, please visit www.nomadicpress.org/submissions

DISTRIBUTION

Orders by trade bookstores and wholesalers:
Small Press Distribution,
1341 Seventh Street
Berkeley, CA 94701
spd@spdbooks.org
(510) 524-1668 / (800) 869-7553

Cryptopedia

This book was made possible by a loving community of chosen family and friends, old and new.

For author questions or to book a reading at your bookstore, university/school, or alternative establishment, please send an email to info@nomadicpress.org.

Cover artwork and author portrait by Arthur Johnstone

Published by Nomadic Press, 111 Fairmount Avenue, Oakland, CA 94611

First printing, 2020

Printed in the United States of America

LIBRARY OF CONGRESS CATALOGING-IN-PUBLICATION DATA

Demcak, Andrew 1968 –
Title: *Cryptopedia*
P. CM.
Summary: *Cryptopedia* by Andrew Demcak speaks directly to the secret sides of our beings, to our shadow-selves. It is the oldest story we have, and it wants to be told. This collection comes from a place where children go missing, where monsters roam freely, and urban myths transform into realities.

[1. POETRY/URBAN MYTH. 2. POETRY/SCIENCE FICTION. 3. AMERICAN GENERAL.] I. III. TITLE.

LIBRARY OF CONGRESS CONTROL NUMBER: 2019957610

ISBN: 978-1-7327866-9-1

Cryptopedia

Andrew Demcak

NOMADIC
PRESS

to my ever-loving husband, Roland:
I love you more than tongue can tell

Attention, my dears:
Let me present you with a story.
It is old and it wants some answers.
This story is in each of us.
I mean you.
I mean me.

– ANNE SEXTON,
"The Gold Key," from
Transformations

CONTENTS

INTRODUCTION

This is a post-post-post-modern book; it is one big metaphor. I reconstructed the poems for *Cryptopedia* using the 1960s cut-up process, or perhaps remix is a better term, that William S. Burroughs used in creating such works as *The Ticket That Exploded* and *Nova Express*, among other novels. My process, however, includes additional poetical steps: editing for meaning/subject matter/clarity, an injection of poetic metrical count (making it, at times, closer to blank verse, or French syllabic verse), and/or insertion various rhyme formulae. This work was created at a time when I was openly rejecting my own earlier "confessional" poetry and was deeply enmeshed in my Master's thesis in Creative Writing at St. Mary's College, Moraga, California. I was focusing on manipulating the "poetic voice."

After I completed my Master's thesis, I began to write what is now *Cryptopedia*, but these poems were very different from my thesis, which dealt primarily with manipulating another writer's voice, not mine. Many of the *Cryptopedia* poems were more like duets between my language and the subject matter. The poems in *Cryptopedia* are cut-ups of Wikipedia articles reconstructed here per its "Fair Use" agreement.

ALIEN HAND SYNDROME, (OR ANARCHIC HAND) *n.*,

She can't distinguish the sensations of her own skin, for example. This patient, case #223, observed leafing site-seeing maps, longing for that first cigarette between her lips. It's to our advantage: we can see her intact, "controlled" hand ("right" meaning "dominant" hand), baffled by the certainty of a tight cashmere glove. The test subject, who had sustained damage to the corpus callosum, when asked, claimed the world was a hoax (see also: split-brain). A clear distinction between muscle, bound to its behaviors, and reflex, seen as "wayward." Notice her drooping forefingers, there in the surveillance photo, limp as birch saplings. The "alien" limb often appears possessed. About twelve minutes into the recent video, the patient's rogue hand moved up to rub out the lit cigarette, but instead, positioned its glowing tip inside her hollow mouth.

ARARAT ANOMALY, *n.*,

Western Plateau, the Turkish/Soviet border. Massif white as Bible paper. A linear facade accumulates glacial ice and frost. Something projected: creaking wood, stranded, or just imagined? Remnants of cleansed pens, mating places? Promulgation of chosen species: squab, pigeon. Do photographs from spy satellites show Noah's timber, or old snowpack, a dove's soul escaping through a keyhole?

THE ARECIBO MESSAGE, *n.*,

Oxygen, phosphorus, and zinc compose DNA. Are we just formulas for sugar and mortality? Which total of nucleotides, a graphic of the double helix, is the human figure? Our message appears in its inscription. We consist of an atomic number, a doorway into the air: hydrogen and black carbon. We sweat, panting in August under the scaffold of planets, our stars singing:

We are here: in the sky, at this place and time, in the fires of despair and ceremony.

The void stands on our shoulders, 1679 binary digits, bytes transmitted by a frequency of phantom hands, reaching upwards, at 2380 MHz. The zeros grinning loops at galaxies, the ones signaling, the fog slinking in, their soliloquy with the night. We worship radio waves from our church seats. The Arecibo's white bell aimed at the M13 star cluster light years away. Dispatch spreading the universe, a salivary hue huffed on glass.

THE BLOOP, *n.*,

Significant, but unexplained, sound. It's more or less gibberish. Perhaps ice calving off Antarctica, or likely animal in origin. The Bloop, its ultra-low frequency, the music of ocean paraphrased. Its source a mystery, much louder than the loudest living creature, our blue whale. The sea makes a submarine's tomb from blur and whorl of benthic volcanoes and hot chemical vents. Is a secret beast catching its kills in the rapid frequency change, in white arcs of amplitude? The abyss inspected, heard on multiple sensors. That liquid note detected several times. Some could call it happy. Autonomous hydrophones listening to the seaweed twisting in dead men's fingers. Situated around 50° S of a submerged coral gnarl, 100° W in a remote point, the hallowed basso.

BRAIN IN A VAT, *n.*,

I am a brain in a vat. The real world is the image of myself in the vat. I've no reference nor reverse evidence. Does shale in the far field flake all morning? Will the earth give its pledge in the flop of wet hooves? Which hidden ores sit in pasture folds? Would the harried creek rush away and be young again? Nerve stimuli are all I know. I am a brain in a vat.

THE BUNNY MAN, *n.*,

Phillips said you donned a doleful gray, black, and white bunny suit. You hacked at a tall porch post with a long-handled knife, saying, "You two people are trespassing! If you don't get the Hell out of here, I'm going to bust both your heads wide open!"

Your stranglehold there. Down the road apiece, they'd discover a blood-encrusted hatchet sunken into a Chevy's side. You couldn't bear the leering driver. "He's got his engine running and that smeared whore in the front seat." They are furtive lovers enticing you to where you saw someone move up and down in the rear window.

Moments later your nylon cord wrapped her throat, the slipknot signed with your teeth, after slinking towards the passenger side, mirror smashed. You answered their white cries with a thrust of your glad blade. Both figures scalped, your furry arms blood-soaked. Police asked the survivor for your description, about the weapon aimed high. You had almost forgotten how your ears kept flopping in the way. It was later confirmed in Fairfax Police records: the car door slapped your hip as you eased around the lifeless girl while the man kept screaming. The pulse of struggle, two lives fixed beneath your fuzzy thumbs.

LAS CARAS DE BÉLMEZ, *n.*,

Allow yourself to focus on the parquet, 1971, in Jaén, Spain. Analyze the molecular changes in the concrete surface: vague suggestions of eyes, a grin appearing, tan skin on the kitchen floor, sensitive, alive as photographic paper; the afterlife's news developing like fresh chromium. The handprint spontaneously formed in the tiling, soiled, soaking in. Witness this in half-light from the windows. Watch your damp footsteps. Observe the woman beneath your sneakers: erotic, her strong figure, as she leans forward, her forearms bleeding faintly, aching, almost alive.

THE CRAWFORDSVILLE MONSTER, *n.*,

There is more to me playing it silent. Infinitesimal and diminishing, the dead boy's last words came. I guessed that he was missing. Who would believe what I saw and not accuse me? It was a beast of no conscience: a flat, oozing creature that resembled a huge amoeba, hovering above the new electric street lamps. Side wings pumping, its exacting mouth wrapped up the delivery boy.

I am bound to report the visible. The creature flapped in front of me like a soft flag. It gave a deep squirm as it fell upon the child who suffered unutterable agony. The great shroud fit itself over the struggling body, pulling him between its lips with propelling fins, and masticated him.

Retribution? There was no tail or head, but it blinked its flaming eyes. I could never explain away what happened to the kid, express a hapless excuse. But it wasn't me. That wheezing, plaintive sound as the fiend was eating. Who sifted facts for the truth, if that someone wasn't me, my brother? Those judges would condemn me; sent to jail by narrow means of one mother's sobbing grief. But I'm innocent.

THE CRYSTAL SKULLS, *n.*,

Mayan descendants left their quartz: twelve skulls plus one arbiter, the original of the Yucatán, containing spirits of ancient humans who had entered to wait for the time when their knowledge was required. The B'ak'tun Calendar, a public memorandum to the earth, an end date, "a death's head made to stop life." Our current timetable, catastrophes, 2021/12/21 disasters: Will thirteen mystical identities forestall this doomsday now predicted, traced back to a defeat of ego?

THE DEVIL'S FOOTPRINTS, [1855], *n.*,

He leaves, wings folded, carrying his harp. *The End.* Footprints appeared far afield, as far south of life as Devon. *Living dream*, my many names for him. I follow the tracks between 80 to 100 miles through a collage of passersby, the insistent flags of cigarette smoke, their bright faces and belongings: old houses, the bent rivers and haystacks, other obstacles I travel straight over, in pursuit. He with his *Book of the Damned* saved, and his footprints left on the tops of snow-covered towns where fear melts to love on the first long roofs and high walls where together we laid.

He still wanders that country. *I love you, Fellow Citizen.* Your dark traces, planted deep and single file, are reported there. You who had stepped from beyond, who arrived to learn the usefulness of white shoelace and ankle bone, come down to me from Dorset. February 1855, our difficult tryst hidden, two men in a snowbank, fresh as flakes. I struggled to find that succession of hoof-like marks in the frost. In these discovered spots, measured nine-inches long, I recall you: your cock and your "demon-like figure." And this amazing want rages through me.

DOPPELGÄNGER EFFECT, *n.*,

My worth is not measured by the ounce. The fatty part still belongs to me. The next electrical stimulation was applied with more intensity while Patient #305 sat up with her arms folded. *I'm staying in school. The future is not known by a magic council.* The patient felt the presence of a "man" who had his arms wrapped around her. *His tarnished hands smother the idea of myself. I kiss his lips in my small mirror.* She described the sensation as highly unpleasant and the electrical stimulation was stopped. *I am always on auction: the arithmetic of the whip judges me.* When the patient was again seated, electric stimulus was applied to the left temporoparietal junction while the patient was asked to perform a language test with a deck of Tarot cards. *Touch me. You'll say I'm golden. I have arrived.* She said the presence was again attempting to interfere with the reading: *He wants to take this card; but he doesn't want me to see it.* On one occasion, the patient reported a sitting person, displaced behind her and to the right. *I weigh in and I am bought. I am summoned here naked.* Similar effects were found for different positions and postures when electric stimulation exceeded 10 mA. *I own the black necklace of fear. I fight against the high bidder in my bloody sleeves.* Again, the effect was disturbing and the electric stimulus ceased.

FERMI PARADOX [OR FERMI'S PARADOX], *n.*,

Let's have it done plum blue: the dank portrait of the world, evolutionary, rogue. A revolutionary step exists between creationism and the paint under a pope's thumbnail. The absence of signs of intelligent beings beyond this planet is a still life *sans* life.

After millions of undercoats, an awkward vertebrate advanced on Earth. The atheist's landscapes suggest few civilizations will colonize space. While a painterly variety of explanations for this paradox exist; the world may be part of a galactic gallery. There goes the Cubist, sort of misguidedly, to demonstrate the hidden universe.

THE GOATMAN, *n.*,

Did you savor the slow-motion grimace of strangers who glimpsed your unshaven face? You wriggled in the yawning woods, but were seen sprinting Centaur-like, alone, at twilight, along Fletchertown's back roads. What of Giles, Goat-Boy, you read about? Did you recall the biotech sweating next to your buzzing incubator lamp? Gone astray, you began attacking staff with your black hooves, each metamorphic phase, your consciousness swelling in reticence. You came back to the lab, an urban myth, to kneel over the lifeless scientist.

THE GREAT THUNDERSTORM, [WIDECOMBE, 1638], *n.*,

The Devil's black horse still tethered to the pinnacle at Widecombe Church. Over the freighted apple orchard, over snow-tipped hedgerows and yew trees, he came like the entering whirl of a thunderstorm. The Devil made a pact with a gambler called Jack Reynolds. If the Devil caught Reynolds asleep in church, he'd come flying, riding solidly, aglow, to collect that card player's soul.

Wind loosed, lightning struck through cloudbank. No comets expected on his surprise visit to the village. The cloven-footed stranger ordered a mug of cider, it hissed as it trickled down his throat. The tankard left a scorch mark on the bar. The landlady found his coins had turned to dried-out leaves. Reynolds nodded off during the sermon. The Devil called on the gambler and carried him off beneath ashen clouds. His last pack of cards thumbed through, their trail left across cumbrous, rain-fêted fields.

THE HIDEBEHIND, *n.*,

Sometimes I sit emptied of the world, my black mood uncurling. I can't be seen directly. My hot targets, including lumberjacks, at my forest table. I dragged them back to my lair to be devoured. I subsist chiefly on their intestines, and I have a severe aversion to alcohol, which I find sufficiently repellent. People disappear into the pines, their plastic boots, white iPads, belts, satin rags, and ashtrays. I am so slender I can easily hide behind any larch trunk. I burn with original hunger. I'm historic. I stop to reconsider events of my day, those nagging problems that sting and sour, after I've gorged myself on hunted honey, a hard-won victim. In folklore, I am allergic to the sun.

IMBUNCHE, *n.*,

Some boys are taken, others sold away. Your captor, Chilote Brujo, a man well-endowed. That first December, the saliva slugged down from his snake tongue. You fiddled the bedspread like medicine. Hoisted up, he touched between your hairs, applied magic cream, finally split your pink hole, side to side. His cock blocked out the moon, transforming the child by breaking each nucleus. Night exhaled smoky ribbons, the stink of a dank well near the swamp. There is something like the edge of a miracle, a second nature, his sticky witchcraft churning through your blood.

THE INTERRUPTED JOURNEY, *n.*,

Cosmic drifts in star charts as reported by Betty Hill: the home planet, number four in the far Zeta Reticuli. Do three Graces haunt these distant spaces? Our futures burn with their airless ardor. But facts of blood support us. Vortex of exhaustion: abducted by aliens. An era's prophesying like protons set ablaze, lighting the reluctant path. What was most extraordinary: their eyes, the irises dark like small birds gleaming with difficult flight. In time, would we gather an answer from that sharpening gaze?

LEYAK, *n.*,

At night, Rangda's head and entrails break loose, the oblique feeling of spirit body. From her hard tongue and fangs come inflections of Balinese on lawns. She demon-howls in bougainvillea, haunts sunken graveyards, feeds upon silky lungfish that bob up like dumplings. Her lewd mask is kept to tease in the village death temple. Harrumphing her poisons, she is paraded. A witch and leyak, a mayfly and child thief, seeking blood under the cover of rain.

M-THEORY, *n.*,

It shepherds those fundamental forces: Einstein's moon, someone's stimulating son, and an improvisation of goldfish splashing in the brisk gravitational state of a canal. Equations describe one grass blade in an untamed forest. The sky as constant. The carrot bisque of our psyche. Childhood, that suffering charge, its restless mass and loss. Electrons and quarks, cloth fedoras to be worn. Today is a symphony of Luna moths.

MAPINGUARI, *n.*,

Vitrine between Brazilian arrowheads and horsehair chairs, the lone mapinguari jiggles its taxidermied bottom, unpacked from a cage-filled backroom, exposed to piggy banks, alarm codes, and combination locks. An exhausted hide to be sold, hauled from a lifetime, sublimed, a dull mummy. The dented spoon of time, long-faced theories of its powerful claws, dusky fur on hind legs. The pawnbroker tiptoes past, matted with guns and pocket knives. Slow, ferocious, its dark shape once prowled the jungle floor beneath the night canopy. Now its lashes tightened around unblinking eyes.

MARKOVIAN PARALLAX DENIGRATE, *n.*,

The random manifestation of words: an open cipher, a steganographic code, or an Internet numbers station? *jitterbugging break caw Newtonian inferring update collaborate rue sportswriting rococo invocate air tousled shadeflower.* Judging by the subject line, the method employs Markov chains, language parsing, and synthetic intelligence. *pathogenesis escritoire novo adventitious most chairperson different pinpoint dunk pendant firelight Pluto.* Usenet, August 5, 1996, two arbitrarily-selected senders "Eric Inhale" and "Glyceride," screens and pages amounting to thousands of email messages with the same timestamp. *episodic medicine ditty crag flogging variac brotherhood file impromptu countenance inheritance.* If Markovian, the communiqué was a signal spies use, the veiled string of numbers, NATO alphabets threaded in the prehistory of Internet. *cohesion yaw refrigerate morphine napkin inland nameable yearbook hark.*

MARY TOFT, *n.*,

"She, being with her first child, took ill and delivered a rabbit. Not person, but clumped fur: one stillborn cottontail. A veil of placenta drawn across it, the Man-Midwife bound up the creature, its tendons cleaned of fat, heart and lungs grown outside its belly, the blood marrows. Mary Toft, a poor woman, trundled it, still weak, choking. She fell aside, seeing the dead animal's unfamiliar limbs. Her claim to have given birth to other mammal parts, as well: shoulders and bent ribs, one violet-colored jaw torn away."

Curtain.

(Her ghastly daydream no longer walled up. The local surgeon looked into the matter: her sly uterus and the pink ribbons of labial flesh. Locals, after all, differed in their opinions: Was Mary Toft a new medical curiosity, fit for The Royal Society? The English woman, from Godalming, Surrey, who in 1726 became pregnant, miscarried bones, hair, and clawed feet.)

MELLIFIED MAN, *n.*,

I'm not found in street markets, an item so extraordinary I commanded a huge price: a Burmese priest, slathered with honey, preserved by liquid coffin. Human contents after centuries, crystalline, transformed into a candy able to heal every ailment. Firstly, my troubled heart collapsed under sugar, then cured to ghost color, in osmosis of such intensity, high acidity, and infective sweetness. The mellification procedure would ideally jelly even these stubborn bones. My donation, I ate just honey, suffused myself with the slick substance. Consider the bees' bright confection as self-sacrifice, hard-spun. My final breath rising out of the golden pool like the sun.

THE MOTHMAN, *n.*,

AFTER E. BISHOP

His wingspan inverted, a flying man electrified by the night. The Mothman revealed. Witnesses insisted, "He doesn't wish to hurt you. He's trying to communicate." But what of the events, the Ohio Mothman fears, people who claimed to have seen this insect falling backward through the air, tiny Icarus, his battered shadow flapping behind him?

The Mothman wanders the horizon's slit, his tear-streaming pupils staring downward. The 1967 collapse of Silver Bridge. The Mothman climbed up it regretfully. Or his death-time when he'll fly into the sun, its small yellow flame at the top of the sky, and immolate himself. He may be investigating his migration route, as skyward as he can soar. Mothman reports arriving from the marble façades. His rare visits to the earth's surface, a moody creature, evening held completely by his dilating eyes.

NACHZEHRER, *n.*,

His tongue fixed in place by copper nail, inhibiting desire. Clumps of dirt under the chin, a white stone as mouth-gag, or a cotton handkerchief tightly wound, choking his throat. Obstacles to prevent his departure from the harboring grave. He shape shifts to a glass tree lit with doves, or a faun thick with mother's milk. Feasting from lust, alongside the glittering pulse of neighborhood blood. A Nachzehrer bathes in night-filtered tombs, coffins upset. Bare, he scavenges like rats in hunger. His mangled cock tip will discover dead boys beneath shrouds of angry tulips.

NECROMANCY, *n.*,

Versed in lifelessness, inaction, decay, time remains unleavened, a grotesque fermented hawk-moth. Its ritual death in a cup of elaborate juice, muscles thrashing circles, the body's mortal end. Or a jury of magic talismans performing the maggot's incantation, a necromancer's weapon, its eggtooth summoning a lapsed spirit. Upon the deceased's eyelids, the widow's prayer, those practiced words which wax in fashions.

NEW MOTIVE POWER, *n.*,

Ushering in a new Utopia, John Spear constructed a mechanical Messiah of copper, zinc, and magnets, all carefully machined for nine months, ritualistically birthed with *tendresse*. The fuddled handful of his followers retreated up the sleeves of a local priest. Spear set to work creating the hallowed "New Motive Power" intended to herald a goldening age.

He believed his tin Apollo, his shining dancer, would be a wakeup call for new technology, beneath Universalist lights of an all-electric church. But instead it turned to stasis, decaying tissue, and the defiant paraphernalia of Spiritualism. He claimed that in his mind's eye he was in contact with "The Guild of Electrizers," a group of anodized spirits including Benjamin Franklin, Thomas Jefferson, and Benjamin Rush. But his omen of Eden faded, blinked out, such a bright moment for a man forsaking his art. And the motionless machine was scrapped, thoroughly dismantled for spare parts.

ORGONOMY, *n.*,

Orgone is oyster gray, raw as the formation of galaxies, of sexuality, whispers ions, bristling bits. Its energy via particulate matter spreading a shoreline. The riptide radiates in the drift of a buoy bell. Those schooners with painted sails at landfall, one flock of sea geese tarrying in the weeds. Cold water pushes the azure rushes, scallop shells amiss. The deep cove alive with the scoot of multitudinous schools, trumpets of anemones, stiff as cocks, diluvian, barnacled like love.

PAREIDOLIA, *n.*,

Macroscopic, the brain understands its baseline. Significant clouds appear in a gazed-at sky. Equally, they are important as anything mankind has made since the Silurian period. Think of the shapes of dogs, dugongs, widowed dinosaurs. These three organisms recorded in a story entitled: "Original Report on the Fossil of Love." Every iota of it is meaningful, in the laboratory that describes you, them, and me, as simple inclusions found in polished limestone.

PONTIANAK, *n.*,

He's pale-skinned, a ghost man in white with fetuses tattooed along his thighs, a Molotov's flame that preys on cheating men, his liquid eyes, black as flax oil. If the silence is broken by dogs' whines, the pontianak must be close behind. Some believe he is called by thumbing holes in filthy underwear, his presence announced by muffled baby cries. He's a tight fist choking the cock, the wet load left in a stack of muscle mags, a lifeless sperm and spit blot, random sex, Friday night, along some regretful road.

QUANTUM IMMORTALITY, *n.*,

The wind twirls a thin stick in the frog pond. Life and death are a dull show. Our theories: the dreams, farthest codas, and transfer maps to numbered planets. Experiments every 10 seconds: the stout figure of a gingko leaf evolved in Earth's spinning.

"Everyone is immortal."

All requisite conditions hinge upon a sequence of binary events. Each street leads us to a quantum end. Here: the mechanics of live death. The whole cosmos disappears, but the experimenter still exists, regardless of how rare the consequence. He dives from the edge of the frozen twig, always iced-over; and the heart of the experimenter, like snow kept in unimaginable heat, survives.

RAWHEAD, *n.*,

Who will be valiant enough to peek through the wallboard crack, glimpse me aglow, bright as a cigarette on a summer night? I am the crouched creature feasting on a pile of loose bones. Children weep when ripe. They smell like briny olives. I'll slap them into subjection; force wide their whining mouths beneath the steady leaves. I live in green ponds; I am Daddy's snake. I curl around tiny necks and drink blood like a 5:15 martini. No one ever gave me anything. If you could get into my brain, you'd know my name: Boogeyman, Mr. Rawhead and Bloody-Bones.

ROKUROKUBI, *n.*,

He sticks his neck out, after a fashion. The sodium street lights blink idly. One blue square of window works the night's hem. iPhones link to editorial blogs. Shoulder pads pillow up, a crazy quilt. The small aims of tee-totaling dandies fit to end it all: stitched majesty of reticulated silk, the stylebook of mortal hazards, foppish in leaky boots, a catwalk loaded with plastic men. He, kinetic model, glimmers, a panache thief. The penis' greasy rigmarole mocks the opulence of his handkerchiefs.

SEDLEC OSSUARY, *n.*,

I chose an enormous chandelier of skeletons, every bone from the body, to hang in the corbeled nave. The skull garlands and desirable ribs draped the vault. My pious act soon spread: A church of Gothic mortar and pale maxilla executed by a half-blind monk of the Cistercian order. Admire it: my white buttresses lifting briefly, zygomatic, the upper chapel in the Czech Baroque style. I employed a stonemason to put the nameless bone heaps into fixed order. This macabre work speaks for itself. Bell-shaped piles of shins occupy the corners. I made every new loss and interment a room. *Fin des temps*, the last task of exhuming carcasses moved many stubborn hooves. But, please, don't thank me. I paused only once during The Black Death's cacophony. Thousands were buried here, confining their histories to chalky mandibles.

SILVERPILEN [LITERALLY, THE SILVER ARROW], *n.*,

Its tracks crossed by the overgrown fence, laden with the drum of train song. Some say the dead get off at Kymlinge. The Silver Arrow train transfers at an ancient stop with no exit. Salvation on Line 1, the abandoned metro hub. Its sides painted by an after-image: one dove. A ghost train lit up by the stars themselves, the thrill and rush of its ethereal passengers, aglow like the lapsed fruit of orchards. Only seen by workers in subway tunnels or passing at high speeds: a shining coffin picking up Stockholm commuters who disappear forever inside the malignant cell of time, or, reappear in the light after *The Light*, arriving always late at night, lost, just in sight of the open-air station.

SKINWALKER RANCH, *n.*,

Old stories: strange strings of UFO lights, invisible objects, the instruments of longing emitting magnetic fields, findings in an unidentified book, animals with glowing red eyes, tongues trilling, uninjured when struck by bright bullets. Investigated phases, evidence of close to fifteen dimensions in West Uintah County, bordering a snip of Ute Indian Reservation. Fifty-year history of weird events: arrays of inexplicable twilights, treed flycatchers, anecdotal sightings of the ring fingers of saints, bigfoot-like creatures, cold crop circles, the art of joy and its lonely bone. From underground labs, journals detail these yearly incidents, the departures of bat wings described by the twitching of six-legged crickets.

THE STARGATE PROJECT, *n.*,

One used a red tarot deck, hunching updates absorbed from the Queen of Cups. "Remote Viewing" is psychological shorthand: thoughts that bounce off of raven wings, clairvoyance, and out-of-body travel. The blood flooding the mind's blotter created a set of live protocols designed to pull out the psychic stops. Stargate got the call after all other intelligence efforts were exhausted, for those midnight scribblers, the lunar machinists, diviners of black pekoe.

THE TOY-BOX KILLER, *n.*,

Understanding is not an antidote. Acknowledge the pig-iron slave collar and exam table nearby where I am padlocked. Today lurches forward on silver pulleys, straps, and flesh clamps. My thighs brushed back, being bodily again, beneath spreader bars, the surgical blades. The youthful man descends, asserts his hands upon me, crossing, pressing.

Who would he be, himself?

In the corner rests someone's meaningless jacket, coiled around a high-heeled shoe. Surge of suffering. He offers me a fist from far across the room. A hidden eyelid swings closed. Perhaps he has a thought, a feeling.

She is not enough for me.

My sodden heap, my flesh, bruises mooning. In vain, one life collected, secret. To him, this workbench is no different from me. His gaze, gleaming, shifts. No bodies were ever found, here, in Truth or Consequences, New Mexico.

THE TUNGUSKA EVENT, *n.*,

Wreckage of an alien vehicle? *I lived in a hut by the river with my young brother, Chekaren. We slept. Suddenly we woke up at the same time.* Finding of quartz slabs with strange hieroglyphs. *We heard whistling and felt a strong wind. Chekaren said, 'Can you hear all those birds flying above?' This was the first thunder.* The explosion in Tunguska, mid-air. *The Earth began to move and shake. Then I saw a wonder: pines were dancing, their branches on fire. It became very bright.* Hills blown down in a hurricane spiral. *How can I say this? It was as if there were a second sun. My eyes were now burning. I even closed them.* After winter, the noticed shine of a spaceship's shell glinting half-buried by thrown debris. *Now I remember well there was also one more thunderclap, but it was so deep and far away, where the sun goes to sleep.*

THE VOYNICH MANUSCRIPT, *n.*,

Those curved arms and centralized hub an antiquarian interpreted as a new galaxy that could only be observed by future telescopes. Other drawings seen as: plant cells through the lens of a microscope? The teasingly obvious Zodiac symbols, and one diagram possibly showing thirteen taffy-colored planets. No one has been able to translate this book's bent glyphs or schematics. A circular image depicts an egg-shaped object sprouting wild roses. To that great alchemy, instructions are inscribed by quilled hand in twisted lines: preparations for medicinal compounds, the role of herb gathering, bloodletting.

This pinpointed machinery: dregs in the offal pit, a girl in bed with birth or rot. Bitter blossoms recognized, each member of the same family: the daisy, the sweet fern, mallow, its calm mother, chamomile. The flower of a river plant really could be the wandering moon in the sky, a composite. Roots of its astral bloom, nib-picked, the white pull of its phases.

11:11 PROMPT, *n.*,

A Pavlovian bell rang where there was no bell. 1,111 Spirit Guardians, called "Midwayers." I've witnessed street lights blinking out while I drove underneath. My ability for pattern recognition. The innate 11:11 prompt, visible signal broadcast through digital watches. A psychic wake-up call on mobile phones. In open places: I am prompted. I can't move the dark lintels of memory, hot circuits in any source of numbers. These unearthly comrades, transcendent, speak to us in that eleventh hour. In the rusted bunker, amazing, I glimpse 11:11 prompts. The air comes full of char and dust, the river of time sweeping away a city burnt to crumbs.

NOTES ON THE POEMS IN *CRYPTOPEDIA*

Alien Hand Syndrome (sometimes used synonymously with anarchic hand) is a neurological disorder in which the afflicted person's hand appears to take on a mind of its own. **Ararat Anomaly** is an object appearing on photographs of the snowfields near the summit of Mount Ararat, Turkey and advanced by some Christian believers as the remains of Noah's Ark. **Arecibo Message** was broadcast into space a single time via frequency modulated radio waves at a ceremony to mark the remodeling of the Arecibo radio telescope on 16 November 1974. **The Bloop** is the name given to an ultra-low frequency and extremely powerful underwater sound detected by the U. S. National Oceanic and Atmospheric Administration (NOAA) in 1997. In philosophy, **The Brain In A Vat** is an element used in a variety of thought experiments intended to draw out certain features of our ideas of knowledge, reality, truth, mind, and meaning. **The Bunny Man** is an urban legend that probably originated from two incidents in Fairfax County, Virginia in 1970, but has been spread throughout the Washington D.C. area. **Las Caras de Bélmez** is an alleged paranormal phenomenon in a private house in Spain which started in 1971 when residents claimed images of faces appeared in the concrete floor of the house. **The Crawfordsville Monster** refers to an alleged creature reported by residents of Crawfordsville, Indiana, in 1891. **The Crystal Skulls** are a number of human skull hardstone carvings made of clear or milky quartz, known in art history as "rock crystal", claimed to be pre-Columbian Mesoamerican artifacts and allegedly possessing mysterious powers. **The Devil's Footprints** is a name given to a phenomenon that occurred in February 1855 around the Exe Estuary in South Devon, England. **Doppelgänger Effect**: In September 2006, it was reported in Nature that Shahar Arzy and colleagues of the University Hospital, Geneva, Switzerland, unexpectedly had reproduced an effect strongly reminiscent of the doppelgänger phenomenon via the electromagnetic stimulation of a patient's brain. **The Fermi Paradox (or Fermi's paradox)** is the apparent contradiction between high estimates of the probability of the existence of extraterrestrial civilization and humanity's lack of contact with, or evidence for, such civilizations. **The Goatman** refers to an urban legend of half-human, half-goat hybrid. **The Great Thunderstorm** (of Widecombe-in-the-Moor in Dartmoor, Kingdom of England), took place on Sunday, 21 October 1638, when the church of St Pancras was apparently struck by ball lightning or a meteor during a severe thunderstorm. **A Hidebehind** is a nocturnal fearsome critter from American folklore that preys upon humans that wander the woods, and was credited for the disappearances of early colonial loggers when they failed to return to camp. According to legend, the **Imbunche** was a male child kidnapped by, or sold by his parents to Brujo Chilote (a type of sorcerer or warlock of Chiloé) as an apprentice and sex partner. **The Interrupted Journey** refers to the story of Betty and Barney Hill, an American couple, who claimed to have been abducted by extraterrestrials in a rural portion of New Hampshire on September 19–20, 1961. In the folklore of Bali, the **Leyak** is a mythological figure in the form of flying head with entrails still attached. A leyak is said to fly around at night trying to find a pregnant woman in order to suck her baby's blood. Rangda is the queen of the leyak. In theoretical physics, **M-Theory** is an extension of string theory in which 11 dimensions are identified. **Mapinguari** is a legendary cryptid said to resemble a ground sloth-like creature with red fur living in the Amazon rainforests of Brazil and Bolivia. **Markovian Parallax Denigrate** refers to a series of articles posted to Usenet on August 5, 1996 consist of what appear to be random words, sometimes numbering in the thousands in a single posting. **Mary Toft** (née Denyer; c. 1701–1763), also spelled Tofts, was an English woman from Godalming, Surrey, who in 1726 became the subject of considerable controversy when she tricked doctors into believing that she had given birth to rabbits and other small animals. **Mellified Man**, or human mummy confection, is a legendary medicinal substance created by steeping a human cadaver in honey. **Mothman** is a legendary creature reportedly seen in the Point Pleasant area of West Virginia from 15 November 1966 to 15 December 1967. Also, a tip of the hat to Elizabeth Bishop's "The Man-Moth". **The Nachzehrer** is prominent in the folklore of the northern regions of Germany, and though officially a vampire, they are also similar to zombies, and in many ways different from either undead. **Necromancy** is a form of magic involving communication with the deceased—either by summoning their spirit as an apparition or raising them bodily—for the purpose of divination, imparting the means to foretell future events or discover hidden knowledge, or to use the deceased as a weapon, as the term may sometimes be used in a more general sense to refer to black magic or witchcraft. John Murray Spear (September 16, 1804–October 5, 1887) was an American Spiritualist clergyman who is most notable for his attempts to construct an electrically powered Messiah which he referred to as the **"New Motive Power."** **Orgonomy** refers to the works of Wilhelm Reich (March 24, 1897–November 3, 1957) an Austrian psychiatrist and psychoanalyst, known as one of the most radical figures in the history of psychiatry. **Pareidolia** is a psychological phenomenon involving a vague and random stimulus (often an image or sound) being perceived as significant. **Pontianak** is a vampiric ghost in Malay and Indonesian mythology, usually depicted as pale-skinned men or women with long hair and dressed in white. They are said to be able to take on any appearance since they prey on unfaithful men. **Quantum Immortality** refers to the subjective experience of surviving quantum suicide regardless of the odds. **Rawhead** is a boogeyman feared by children, and is sometimes called Bloody-Bones, Tommy Rawhead, or Rawhead and Bloody-Bones. **Rokurokubi** are demons found in Japanese folklore. They look like normal human beings by day, but at night they gain the ability to stretch their necks to great lengths. They can also change their faces to those of terrifying oni to scare mortals. **The Sedlec Ossuary** in the Czech Republic is estimated to contain the skeletons of between 40,000 and 70,000 people, whose bones have been artistically arranged to form decorations and furnishings for the chapel. **Silverpilen**, literally The Silver Arrow, is the nickname of a Stockholm Metro train which features in several urban legends all alleging the sighting of the train's "ghost." **Skinwalker Ranch**, also known as Sherman Ranch, is a property located on approximately 480 acres southeast of Ballard, Utah that is allegedly the site of paranormal and UFO-related activities. **The Stargate Project** was the umbrella code name of one of several sub-projects established by the U. S. Federal Government to investigate claims of psychic phenomena with potential military and domestic applications, particularly "remote viewing": the purported ability to psychically "see" events, sites, or information from a great distance. **Toy-Box Killer** is a reference to David Parker Ray (November 6, 1939–May 28, 2002) a suspected American serial killer and known torturer of women. **The Tunguska Event** was an enormously powerful unexplained explosion that occurred near the Podkamennaya Tunguska River in what is now Krasnoyarsk Krai, Russia, at about 7:14 a.m. KRAT (0:14 UT) on June 30 [O. S. June 17], 1908. **The Voynich Manuscript**, described as "the world's most mysterious manuscript", is a work which dates to the early 15th century, possibly from northern Italy. **11:11 Prompt**: "These 11:11 wake-up calls on your digital clocks, cell phones, DVD players and microwaves are the "trademark" prompts of a group of just 1,111 fun-loving Spirit Guardians, or Angels, and the 11:11 prompt is their way of using our innate ability for pattern recognition to let us know that they are here." From the website *www.1111angels.net*

CLASSROOM GUIDE

Below, please find a few questions to consider when teaching *Cryptopedia* in the classroom:

- What are the themes and connections that run through *Cryptopedia*?
- What do you think the author, Andrew Demcak, is trying to communicate with *Cryptopedia*'s triangular back and forth between scientific ideas, religious figures, and mythological or folkloric creatures?
- Many of the pieces in *Cryptopedia* deal with absence, both domestic and cosmological, or hidden threats and unexplained conspiracies or myths. What is Demcak saying about things which are missing or things which are hidden or secret?
- Is Demcak saying that there is a connection between what we call "Religion (or Magic)" and what we call "Science?"
- What place do the poems about children occupy in *Cryptopedia*?

ACKNOWLEDGEMENTS

My humble thanks to Natasha Dennerstein for suggesting I submit my work to Nomadic Press, and to everyone at Nomadic Press for making this such a fantastic journey, especially J. K. Fowler.

Thank you to the following publications, where some of these pieces first appeared: "Arecibo Message" appeared in *Knockout Literary Magazine*; "The Crawfordsville Monster," "Las Caras de Bélmez," "Markovian Parallax Denigrate," "Orgonomy," and "The Toy-Box Killer," were published in the online literary journal *Spork*; "Rawhead" appeared as a video/poem at PoetsArtists.com.

ANDREW DEMCAK is an American poet and novelist and the author of five poetry collections and seven Young Adult/New Adult novels. His books have been featured by The American Library Association, Verse Daily, The Lambda Literary Foundation, The Best American Poetry, and Poets and Writers. His first book of poetry, *Catching Tigers in Red Weather* (Three Candles Press, 2007), was selected by Joan Larkin to win The Three Candles Press "Open Book Award." He has also been a finalist for the prestigious Dorset Poetry Prize, the Gloria E. Anzaldúa Poetry Prize, The Crazyhorse Poetry Award, and the Louise Bogan Award for Artistic Merit and Excellence in Poetry.